One

Deep in the woods of Hilton in the Hollow, Wolfie T. Volfango lay in his sleeping bag and read, for the one hundred and tenth time, the letter that had brought him to England. It was from his aunt. This is what it said:

Dear Wolfie,

I want you to pay me a visit in Olde England. Travel broadens the mind,

Wolfie, and if yours is anything like your mother's, it will need all the help that it can get.

I myself will not be free to show you round, owing to a grave miscarriage of justice. Luckily, my old friend Gussie Godiva will. She runs the Post Office at Hilton in the Hollow, which is a lovely spot, and just the place for you to start your holiday.

While you are there, Wolfie, I very much hope that you will meet a child called Dimanche Diller. Dimanche is an orphan, Wolfie, and you know you should be extra kind to orphans, don't you?

If you take Dimanche on a little outing, her rich aunt will be most grateful to you, when you bring her back. And so will I.

Do what I ask, Wolfie, and when I come out – which will be in approximately 1,725 days – I will repay your kindness.

Your loving Aunt Valburga.

PS If you come to England and look for Dimanche, I will pay for your ticket on the plane.

PPS Plus expenses.

PPPS Plus a salary. A big one, Wolfie.

The prison officer whose job it was to read the prisoners' letters was deeply moved by such kind intentions.

"Just fancy that old baggage treating her nephew to a free trip over here, and thinking of ways to make a little orphan happy," he said to his mate Stan. He shed a tear, and so did Stan. They agreed that the power of prison to reform even the worst of criminals was truly remarkable.

Wolfie was moved by the letter too. He didn't get many, and he took this one very seriously, especially the PSs. He hurried to the airport and caught the first plane east – which is how he came to be sitting opposite his Aunt Valburga on a hard chair in the visitor's room of HM Prison The Vaults. Prison visiting rooms, as you'll know if you've been in one, can be noisy places. This one was. It was absolutely full of visiting husbands, fathers, aunts and uncles, friends and relations. Above all it was full of dozens of visiting children, all falling off their chairs, and spilling their drinks down one another's necks, and nicking each other's crisps, and running up and down and being shouted at. It was quite easy for Wolfie's aunt to tell him her plan without being overheard, and that is what she did. Slowly and carefully.

"Repeat after me," she whispered, when she had finished.

"After me," Wolfie T. Volfango murmured obediently.

Valburga closed her eyes. "Idiot! Start again. Tell me exactly what you've got to do!"

"OK, Auntie, keep your shirt on. I got to kidnap the kid and keep her hid. I got to not let her go till her auntie dishes the dough."

"Good, Wolfie! And where are you going to hide the little so-and-so?"

"Out in the woods."

"Good, Wolfie. And who do you get the ransom from?"

"From her auntie, the nun at the big house."

"Good, Wolfie. And what do you do with the ransom when you've got it?"

"I keep it safe for when you come out, Auntie."

"Good, Wolfie. And when will that be?"

"One thousand seven hundred and twenty-five days, Auntie. Unless you dig your way out first."

"Don't be ridiculous, Wolfie."

A noisy buzzer marked the end of visiting time. All over the room visitors hugged their loved ones, and their loved ones hugged them back. Well, almost all over the room – it would have taken a braver man than Wolfie to hug Valburga Vilemile.

In fact Wolfie felt downright grateful to the buzzer. He got to his feet and shook hands with his aunt.

"Mind you do exactly what I've told you, Wolfie," Valburga said.

Wolfie looked at Valburga. Deep in his chest a voice woke up and murmured something.

"You ain't got to do what she tells you to, Wolfie baby," it said.

"Aw, shuddup!" Wolfie replied. He wasn't

used to listening to his conscience. In fact this may have been the very first time it had ever spoken to him.

Two

Two days later Wolfie strolled up to the Post Office of Hilton in the Hollow. He pushed open the door, making Gussie Godiva's little bell ring merrily.

Gussie looked up from behind the counter, adjusted her monocle, and stared hard at Wolfie. Then she walked right up to him, reached a skinny arm behind him, and flipped the sign on the Post Office door from OPEN to CLOSED.

It is against the law to shut a Post Office in

the middle of the morning, but Gussie Godiva was not interested in the law. She was interested in Wolfie T. Volfango.

She had not met Wolfie before, but she recognized him immediately from the photograph his aunt had sent her. It wasn't difficult.

Wolfie had the sort of head that makes you think of a Dutch cheese – round, and smooth, and shiny. His ears hung low on either side of it like two soft folds of dough. His beady eyes peeped round his nose like tiny, startled creatures round a rock, and to the south of them his teeth jostled for space. Lower still his great jaw surged forward in a rippling cliff of bone, bypassing his neck and merging with his powerful shoulders.

Wolfie greeted Gussie Godiva politely. He gave her a box of chocolates and a letter from his aunt. Gussie dropped the chocs into her knitting bag and read the letter carefully. She read it again. Then she took Wolfie through into her back room and offered him a cup of tea.

"I've tried your English tea, Ma'am. Could I have a cold beer, please?"

"I don't believe in offering young people strong drink, young man."

"Beer ain't strong drink, Ma'am."

"It is in my book. And anyway I haven't got any. I keep a herbal decoction in the cupboard, but that is for medicinal purposes only."

Wolfie was surprised to hear this. He could smell something on Gussie Godiva's breath, and he did not think it was medicine.

"Your aunt tells me she has a job for you to do, my boy. She says in this letter that she's told you all about it."

Wolfie nodded unhappily.

"She wants me to help you with it, Wolfie."

"Yes, Ma'am."

"You do know what the job is, don't you?"

"Yes, Ma'am."

"And are you confident of being able to fulfil your aunt's wishes, Wolfie?"

"Do what, Ma'am?"

"Can you do the job, boy?"

"I could, Ma'am."

"Excellent, Wolfie."

'But I don't want to."

"Why ever not?"

"Cause it's against the law, Ma'am."

"Stupid boy! Of course it isn't! The laws here are quite different from those in America. Your aunt is an old school friend of mine, Wolfie. I've known her all my life. You surely cannot think that she would ask you to do anything illegal? In any case, your aunt and I are perfectly capable of dealing with the law. Don't worry your head about it. Your job, Wolfie, is to do exactly what you're told."

The voice in Wolfie's chest tried to speak to him again at this point, but once again he ignored it.

"Now, let's run through your aunt's plan step by step," Gussie continued firmly.

"All right, Ma'am. But I don't like it."

When Gussie Godiva had finished, Wolfie still didn't like it. But he was used to being bossed. His mother, back in Pasadena, Texas, was bossy. All her friends were bossy, too. Over the years Wolfie had grown used to ignoring his own ideas and doing what he was told. This is not good for anyone. It can lead to all sorts of trouble, and this time it did.

After Wolfie had left the Post Office, Gussie poured herself a sloe gin, took out a quill pen, dipped it into a bottle of green ink, and wrote the following letter to Valburga:

My dear Valburga,

Your nephew Wolfie called on me today. The boy's a selfish blighter and I'm sure he won't share the loot unless he's forced to. I doubt if he'll even get his fat hands on it without my help.

What a pity that you can't be here to keep an eye on him. Young people are so unreliable, aren't they? But you can rely on me to make him do exactly what he's told.

I'm sure you will reward me generously. Shall we say 50% to me and 25% each to you and Wolfie? I understand you want Wolfie to take the orphan on a boat trip – I will deduct the cost of this from your share.

All the best,

Your old chum,

Gussie.

PS On second thoughts how about
60-20-20?

PPS How about 70-30 and we skip Wolfie?

Gussie Godiva addressed the letter to Prisoner
number 4,723, c/o HM Prison The Vaults,
Wold-under-Water, and posted it with a first
class stamp on in her own letter box.

Three

Rain soaked the woods and fields of Hilton in the Hollow, and overhead, a chilly wind drove heavy clouds across the sky. Sister Verity sat in the cosy drawing-room of Hilton Hall with her soft black habit tucked round her ankles, and worked on her embroidery. Every now and then she smiled at her niece Dimanche, who sat on the floor surrounded by sheets of paper, with a pencil in one hand and a rubber in the other.

Dimanche was designing a two-storey tree house to be built in the tulip tree on the lawn. She had sketched in the main load-bearing branches of the tree, and made notes of how she wanted the two storeys to fit together. Now she was trying to work out how much wood she'd need for the first platform.

Cosmo Cockle, the gardener, had promised her an old door and a pile of planks. His fiancée Polly, who had been Dimanche's nanny until Sister Verity came, had promised her a pair of folding wooden steps and an old wooden clothes horse. Both would come in handy, and the steps might even make a ladder between the two floors of the house.

"I'll need more wood, Aunt Verity," she said. "But I can't work out how much."

"Neither will I be able to," Sister Verity replied. "You know I can't do sums. But Polly will. She's brilliant at them."

"I'll ask her. But now I want to go outside. I've got pins and needles from sitting down too long."

"Where will you go, Dimanche?"

"Just out. Would you like to come too?"

"Not this time. I promised the Sisters I'd

have this altar cloth ready for Easter, and I've still got five pansies and a caterpillar left to do."

Sister Verity had left her convent in France to care for Dimanche, but she still wore her habit, and sent all sorts of gifts to the Sisters. She planned to rejoin them one day, when Dimanche should have no further need of her. The altar cloth she was making showed a whole orchard in blossom, all sewn in tiny, perfect feather-stitch, and bordered with wild pansies. Sainte Gracieuse had been famous throughout Normandy for her love of cider. And although she was a noted apple-grower herself, the saint had always had a soft spot for caterpillars and other pests, so Sister Verity generally included one or two in her embroideries.

"You go if you like, Dimanche. But don't go near the river, will you? It's bound to be flooded after all the rain we've had. And I think that you should wear your mackintosh."

Actually, it was the river that interested Dimanche. She wanted to see the underwater fields, with the trees sticking up out of the flood, and all the banks washed away. But she was far too thoughtful to say so to her aunt Verity, who would certainly have worried if she had.

Dimanche put on her gumboots and mackintosh and set off along the path through the damson trees and out into the valley. She put her hands in her pockets and felt her silver-handled penknife. She had found it in the attic, and treasured it because it had once belonged to her father. She took it out, and began to whittle a stick with its sharp blade. Her curly dark hair was soon glittering with raindrops. They flew out in a sparkling wreath each time she jumped a ditch, and her brown eyes scanned the stormy woods and fields with pleasure as she drew nearer to the river. She did not see Wolfie T. Volfango, squinting down the sights of his Rapid Action Night Sight Self-Aiming Mighty Hunter Bow and Arrow Set.

Seen through its sights, Dimanche looked like a small ghost, wavering and bobbing across an invisible meadow. Wolfie watched her intently, breathing heavily because of the concentration this required. He wondered about the best way to capture her. He could see by the lively way she sloshed along that it would not be easy.

One hour later, deep in the woods, Wolfie baled out his all-seasons sleeping bag and prepared for another wet night. "I'll dig a pit," he decided. "That's what I'll do. I'll dig a pit, and cover it over with branches, like they do in books. Then I'll wait till she falls in."

He took a strip of biltong from his backpack and began to chew. He did not like biltong, but he ate it all the same, because he knew it was the sort of thing a rough, tough soldier of fortune should eat. He chewed for a while, and spat. He adjusted the oilskin shelter he had rigged up over his dug-out, and pulled his wet blanket round his shoulders. Rain drummed noisily on the roof, making sleep impossible.

Wolfie tried to think pleasant thoughts, to make up for the dreadful weather. He thought about the money he was going to get from his aunt. Would it be enough for flying lessons? Enough to buy a helicopter of his own? Or maybe a small fixed-wing plane? A glider would do, he thought, or a micro-light or a hot-air balloon. He didn't care, as long as he got airborne.

Many people have a saving grace, if only you can find it, and it is a strange fact of life that a person's saving grace can often be their downfall. That's how it was for Wolfie. Wolfie was hooked on flying. The very first time he'd watched a tiny silver needle stitch across the Pasadena sky, he had longed to fly. When he boarded the jet to fly to England and felt the mighty throb and surge of the engines, felt himself lifted clear of the earth and thrown into the sky, he was hooked. The plane trembled, just for a second, before jumping off the runway and into the air, and in that second Wolfie was in heaven. For the first time he understood, really understood, the astonishing fact that the sky starts where the earth leaves off. There, just above the runway, Wolfie sensed the wonder and the mystery of aerodynamics.

So you see, there was no chance for goodness to triumph over evil. Not straight away, at any rate. Wolfie knew, without even thinking about it, that he was going to kidnap Dimanche and hold her to ransom. He also knew he wasn't going to let his aunt get her hands on the ransom money. Not if he could help it.

Which is why Wolfie lay alone in the wet woods of Hilton in the Hollow, making aeroplane noises to blot out the creepy sounds that filled the darkening wood, making him think of ghosts. Eyes shut, fingers in ears, he rocked gently under his tarpaulin, dreaming of the wide blue yonder.

Every now and then visions of money floated through his brain. "Grab the kid," he murmured to himself. "Grab the kid and keep her hid, Wolfie baby. Nothing to it."

Dimanche, rounding a bend in the woodland path as she hurried homewards after a satisfying splash in the Fenny, tripped right over Wolfie T. Volfango as he sat with his eyes shut, making aeroplane noises. It gave them both a nasty fright.

Wolfie leapt up, fell over, and scrambled out of his sleeping bag. He threw it over Dimanche's head. Poor Dimanche was pinned to the ground by yards of billowing duckdown. Smothered, amazed, and terrified, she did the only thing she could. She bit the hand which Wolfie had clamped over her mouth. It tasted awful but it did the trick. Wolfie whipped his hand away and stared in horror at the tooth marks Dimanche had left in his skin.

"You didn't ought to bite people!" he said, letting go of Dimanche and beginning to suck his hand. "It ain't nice manners."

One second later Dimanche was hurtling back down the path. Wolfie stared after her. What he saw disappearing round the corner was not a frightened child. It was flying lessons. It was an aeroplane of his own. It was everything he wanted in the world. He lurched to his feet and took off after her.

Dimanche heard Wolfie's uneven steps behind her. She heard him panting as he gained on her. She ran, and ran faster. But Wolfie caught her easily. Once bitten, twice shy, they say. He knocked her down, picked her up, and threw her over his shoulder like a sack of beans. Then he set off at a steady lope between the dripping trees.

Wolfie was heading for a secret place his aunt had told him about, a place she said was ideal for keeping prisoners in. He didn't feel the least bit guilty – he just could not believe his luck. His aunt had warned him that Dimanche was a brainy child and would be hard to catch. Now, here she was, his prisoner. And all without him having to lift a finger, never mind dig a pit.

Dimanche meanwhile was doing her best to work out where she was being carried off to. It wasn't easy, head down and bouncing, but Dimanche didn't give up easily. Presently she noticed that the trees were thinning out. She recognized the road to Rockford Market. It looked different upside down.

Dimanche knew that Tom Shovel would be cycling down that very road quite soon, on his way to visit his friend Lucasta Lovelace for their weekly game of Scrabble. I must leave him a clue, she thought. So people will know where to start looking for me.

She held her precious penknife tightly in her hand. She knew that she must time it right. The knife must fall on the road, not into the long grass or the ditch, or there would be no hope of Tom Shovel spotting it from his bike.

It wasn't easy, slung over Wolfie's shoulder, bumping and thumping with every step he took, to drop the penknife at exactly the right moment. It wasn't easy to let it fall, to drop it as if it were nothing, instead of being something that reminded her of her father, something she had treasured since first it came into her hand. But Dimanche managed it.

Looking back, she could see the little knife gleaming like a tiny drop of light on the road for a second. Then it disappeared as Wolfie carried her further away.

Tom Shovel will see it, Dimanche told herself. He'll see it and he'll pick it up. He'll know it's mine, he's seen me fiddling with it a hundred times, and sharpened it for me on his whetstone often. He'll take it to Aunt Verity, and she'll call the police, and they'll organize a band of volunteers to look for me. Everyone'll help. They're bound to find me. Aren't they?

Dimanche knew the woods round Hilton Hall better than Wolfie did because of all the happy hours she had spent climbing trees and building dens in them. But she did not know every single nook and cranny of them, and when Wolfie stopped at last, it was in a place that she had never seen before. The big old oak trees had grown fewer and further between. Dense low hollies made a sort of hedge through which Wolfie pushed, prickling poor Dimanche dreadfully. Beyond the holly hedge lay an overgrown field of docks and ragwort, and at the far side of the field slouched a tumbledown shack of brick and slate. Its cracked and dirty windows winked in the light of the rising moon.

"This is where I'm going to hide you," Wolfie announced with pride. "What do you reckon?"

Dimanche did not reply.

* * *

Back on the Rockford Market road, Tom Shovel pedalled slowly towards Lucasta Lovelace's house, talking quietly to himself. "Xmas," he murmured. "Xebec, Xenon. Yak, yam, yell. Zeal, zinc, zone, zoom, zygote. Huzza. Hymnal. Quoth. Quoin. Quoit. I'll beat you this time, Lucasta Lovelace!"

He did not see Dimanche's little knife, winking in the moonlight by the side of the road.

Four

"Are you OK?" grunted Wolfie as he lowered Dimanche to the floor of the charcoal-burner's shack. It was the first time he'd kidnapped anyone, and he felt a bit embarrassed. Dimanche began to cry.

"Hey! Don't!" Wolfie begged. "Please don't!" But Dimanche did. If Wolfie had said something unpleasant to her, she might never have started. But he didn't, and now she couldn't stop.

"Ain't you got a handkerchief?" Wolfie asked.

Dimanche shook her head. Wolfie would have liked to lend her his, but it was much too dirty. "I'm only holding you to ransom, kid," he said. "It ain't gonna hurt."

Dimanche went on crying. Wolfie felt more and more upset. If she didn't stop soon, he thought, he might start crying himself.

"All I'm gonna do is keep you hid till your rich auntie pays me a ransom. After that I'll let you go. I've got food here for you to eat, and a pile of my best comics that I'll let you read. So turn off the waterworks."

"My aunt will never give in to blackmail!" Dimanche said fiercely – though secretly, she couldn't help hoping that Sister Verity would. She began to cry harder.

"I can't let you go, kid," said Wolfie, miserably. "It ain't up to me. I've got to get the money off your aunt to give to MY aunt."

This wasn't strictly true, of course, because Wolfie had decided to keep the money for himself and spend it on flying lessons, or a private plane, or both. And he was being paid to carry out the kidnap too. But the thought of making Dimanche cry so as to get something nice for himself made him feel terribly uncomfortable.

"You don't know my aunt," he said. "But if you did, you wouldn't want to cross her. When she gets angry, everybody suffers." He took a length of rope from behind the door and began to tie Dimanche up.

Just at first, being tied up by Wolfie did not frighten Dimanche all that much. She was sure he'd be no good at knots and she planned to wriggle free the moment he took his eyes off her and make another dash for freedom. What she had not taken into account, because she did not know it, was that Wolfie T. Volfango had been a boy scout.

If there is one thing boy scouts are good at, it's knot work. Wolfie knew how to tie bowlines and sheepshanks and clove hitches and bloodknots. He had won prizes with his macramé when he was just a cub scout. What Wolfie didn't know about knots, no scout would bother with. Dimanche soon realized that she was up against an expert.

"Listen," she said, as Wolfie worked on his knots. "Kidnapping is a serious crime. You're bound to be caught, and you'll get into awful trouble."

Wolfie paused halfway through a sheepshank.

"It wasn't my idea," he muttered.

"Even if that's true, it won't cut any ice with the judge. In the eyes of the law you are a kidnapper and I wouldn't like to be in your shoes when they catch you. You'll go to prison for years and years. Do you know what it's like in prison?"

"Yes," said Wolfie. "My auntie's in one, and I went to visit her. She's the one who told me to kidnap you."

"That's *terrible!*" Dimanche exclaimed. "Your own aunt told you to commit a crime! She must be horrible!"

"She sure is."

"Then you're crazy to do what she says!"

"She told me it wouldn't do no harm. She said it weren't against the law in England, only in the USA."

"And you believed her?"

"Aunties don't tell lies."

"Yours does. Anyway, how could you agree to do anything so mean? Haven't you got a mind of your own? Don't you feel guilty?"

All of a sudden, Wolfie did.

"Just think what *my* aunt, who's kind and loves me, is going through right now! You ought to be ashamed of yourself!" Wolfie began to cry. Dimanche stopped.

"Look, I didn't mean to upset you, Wolfie," she said. "But surely you can see that you must let me go?"

Wolfie shook his head. "I can't."

"Why not?"

"I'm scared of my auntie."

"Don't be such a baby, Wolfie."

"I can't help it."

Poor Wolfie couldn't. And there was worse to come. While he sat wondering what to do to put things right, and thinking that he *could* not, just could *not* give up the chance of flying lessons and a plane of his own, a storm was blowing up outside the charcoal-burner's shack. Rain poured across the slate roof and spattered down the chimney. It sluiced over the windows and drummed on the door. Darkness wrapped round the little house, turning the night outside into an enemy.

A loose slate slid off the roof and smashed onto the doorstep. At the same moment a branching spear of lightning shot down from sky to earth, followed a split second later by a rip of thunder. Wolfie let out a moan of fear and crept under the table. Sensing that she was about to get the upper hand, Dimanche took a deep breath.

"Wolfie. I can understand that you might be too scared of your aunt to let me go free. Because I can see you're a bit of a coward. But I don't believe that you're a bad person at heart, are you?"

Wolfie did not reply. He was trying to hide from the lightning by pulling his mighty hunter hat down over his eyes.

"Listen to me, Wolfie. You must take a letter from me to my Aunt Verity. You must leave it on the doorstep at Hilton Hall and ring on the doorbell. Hide behind the hedge until someone comes out and picks it up. After that, you can come back here."

"Why should I do all that for you?" Wolfie asked miserably.

"Because in return, I promise I'll do three things for you. I promise I won't try to escape while you're away. I promise that when you're caught – and you will be caught – I'll tell the judge you took a message for me, even though you're scared of thunder. That ought to count for something. And I promise to visit you in prison and be your friend. If you take the letter for me, Wolfie. Will you do it?"

There was a long silence – if you don't count thunder and lightning – during which Wolfie continued to sit under the table with his hat pulled well down, not saying anything.

"I don't suppose anybody else will visit you. Prison can be a very lonely place, Wolfie. Will you do it?"

"Nope."

"Nope? What d'you mean, *nope*?"

"I mean I won't do it."

"You *must*!"

"I don't must."

"You *do* must!"

"Nope, I don't must."

"Wolfie. Think about it. If you do this thing, it will be a brave and good thing that you're doing."

"I don't care."

"Wolfie, you do. Deep in your heart, you want to be brave and good. And for people to know that you are. A lot of people. People who'll say: 'Wow, that Wolfie is brave and good.' People who'll say: 'Well, he may have done what his aunt told him to do, and he should have known better, but all the same, when it came to the crunch, Wolfie T. Volfango did the right thing. That Wolfie T. Volfango is a hero!'"

Perhaps Dimanche did lay it on a bit thick, but it worked. At the word hero, Wolfie peeped out from underneath the table.

"Me? A hero?" he asked.

"Yes, Wolfie! You!"

"How would people know what I done, Dimanche?"

"It would be in all the papers, Wolfie."

"Would it?"

"Sure to be! Think about it, Wolfie. LONE MAN BATTLES THROUGH STORM! BRAVE YOUNG WOLFIE RISKS ALL TO SET AN ANXIOUS AUNTIE'S MIND AT EASE. They might take your picture too. You would be famous, Wolfie."

This was too much for Wolfie. Who does not want to be famous?

"I'll do it!" he shouted.

It was a turning point in his life. It was the first time anyone had asked him to do something brave and selfless, and it made him see himself in a new light. No more Wolfie the Stupid, Wolfie the Dumb, Wolfie who Nobody Liked. From now on he would be Wolfie the Bold! Wolfie the Kind! Wolfie the Hero! "I'll do it!" he shouted again, and all at once he felt quite proud.

Dimanche almost began to cry again, this time with relief. Things are not always as bad as they seem, she told herself. She smiled, and Wolfie, thinking the smile was for him, smiled back.

Neither of them would have been smiling had they known what Wolfie's aunt was doing at that very moment.

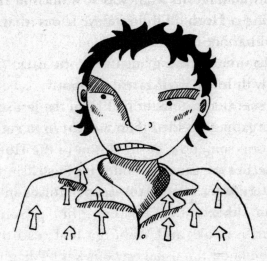

Five

Twenty miles south of Hilton in the Hollow a tall, forbidding building flickered in the intermittent flashes of white light.

Deep down underneath the wretched courtyard where the prisoners took their dreary exercise, Valburga Vilemile sweated and dug in the wet earth.

She did not like her nephew. Ever since their meeting in the noisy visiting room, she had doubted his ability to carry out her plan. And if he did manage it, what was to stop him from running off with all the money? It was what she would have done herself.

"He would!" she grunted, as she dug. "The greedy little sap would steal my loot!"

Gussie Godiva's letter had been the last straw. Valburga had decided then and there to get out of prison somehow, go to Hilton in the Hollow, and secure the ransom money for herself.

There were plenty of escape stories in the prison library. They were the prisoners' favourite books and Valburga had read them all. She knew the usual way out was by digging a tunnel.

The first thing to do was to get her bunk bed moved, and that wasn't difficult. She made herself stay awake for several nights by listing her enemies alphabetically. When she had developed good heavy bags under both eyes, she mentioned to her warder that she was developing a bad case of insomnia. "Which as you know," she added, "can lead straight to insanity and death."

It can't, but the warder didn't know that. He was a friendly soul, who had ended up in his present job quite by accident, and didn't much enjoy it. When Wolfie's aunt said she thought she'd sleep better if she could move her bed next to the tiny window, against the outside wall of her cell, he readily agreed.

The second part of the plan involved Wolfie's aunt behaving abnormally well for a long time. This was much more difficult, but she did it, and was rewarded with permission to work on the prison farm, a favourite job with all the prisoners.

Wolfie's aunt was issued with a pair of gumboots and a spade and told to dig potatoes. By day she dug potatoes, and by night she dug a tunnel, starting under her bed. She soon worked out a way of hiding the spare earth from the tunnel inside her gumboots, and emptying it out on the potato patch each day. She developed powerful muscles what with digging day and night, and mud pies formed inside her gumboots, but she didn't care.

Six

Inside the charcoal-burner's shack, Wolfie T. Volfango produced a stub of pencil from his pocket, ripped a bit off the back of an old comic, and handed both to Dimanche.

Dimanche thought for a moment. Then she wrote:

Am safe and well, but have been captured.
Try not to worry.
Love, Dimanche.

She took a precious pendant from round her neck – it was a silver one her aunt had given her – and wrapped it in the note. Then she gave both of them to Wolfie.

"Can't I wait until the thunder's stopped?" Wolfie asked hopefully.

"I'm afraid not. It's getting worse, and you don't want to have to be even braver, do you? Go now, and don't stumble into the river by mistake. It'll be well and truly flooded."

The next hour was a long one for Dimanche, alone in the deserted shack. It was not pleasant to sit on the old kitchen chair, tied securely by a round turn and two half hitches, and listen to the howling of the storm. Eerie white lightning continued to flicker. Rain on the window distorted the trees as they struggled and thrashed in the gale. An old rose bush tore loose from the wall and tap-tapped at the door, making Dimanche think of bony fingers.

Each time the thunder cracked she jumped as much as you can jump when you're tied to a chair, and she could not help imagining what would happen if the roof was struck by lightning or a flying thunderbolt. Sometimes a strong imagination is a blessing. This time it wasn't.

A few tears trickled down Dimanche's nose and plopped onto the table. She twisted her head round to wipe her nose on her shoulder, and as she did so, she noticed a movement at the window.

Two big eyes, crazy and round and yellow, were staring in at her. A death-coloured face hovered just outside the window. It moved oddly, seeming to dip and weave. Rain spattered on the glass and the face dissolved, only to reassemble a second later like the pattern in a kaleidoscope. Dimanche let out a scream of horror. The death face answered with a screech. Silent wings spread wide, pale feathers scraped against the window, and Dimanche glimpsed the lovely swoop of a barn owl as it vanished into the dark woods.

The worst of her fear went with it, but it left her feeling weak with shock, and dreadfully alone. A little comforting memory crept into her frightened mind – another time, another owl, a tiny ball of cream-coloured fluff like a bedraggled meringue, asleep inside the cold frame.

"Followed a mouse in there, I dare say," Cosmo had explained. "Ate it up and fell asleep, most likely."

Dimanche had eased the lid of the cold frame open and gently lifted the owlet out. It had nestled in the palm of her hand for a second, blinking in the unexpected daylight. The memory of its feathers, soft against her palm, made Dimanche feel a little less alone.

Perhaps it was just as well she did not know that even as the owl floated away through the storm-torn woods, Wolfie's cruel aunt was climbing triumphantly out of the mouth of a muddy tunnel and setting off with steady strides towards the charcoal-burner's shack.

Seven

Wolfie crouched in the rhododendrons outside Hilton Hall. Rain trickled down his neck, making him feel less of a hero than he had when he was with Dimanche. Nobody seemed to have heard the doorbell. He rang again.

Five minutes later he heard footsteps, and a yellow line appeared under the door. It opened to reveal Sister Verity, with Polly by her side. Both of them stared anxiously out into the night. They longed to see Dimanche come marching in out of the storm, but nobody was there. Verity was about to shut the door when she noticed a crumpled piece of paper lying on the doorstep. She bent and snatched it up. Out of it, to her amazement, fell Dimanche's silver pendant!

Smoothing out the crumpled note Verity read it, quickly at first and then again, slowly. She held both note and pendant tightly to her bosom and folded herself into Polly's arms. The two of them turned slowly round on the brightly lit doorstep like little figures in a musical box.

Out in the darkness, Wolfie watched. Would anybody ever be so glad that he was safe, he wondered? The door closed, shutting in the warm light and the embracing women, and Wolfie turned sadly away.

Inside Hilton Hall, Polly and Sister Verity comforted one another.

"Cheer up, Sister Verity," murmured Polly. "I'd like to see the kidnapper that could get the better of Dimanche."

"You're right, as usual," smiled Sister Verity. "And at least we know that she's alive. That's something to be thankful for. I shall telephone the police at once and ask for their help."

A short while later, Chief Inspector Barry Bullpit was calling up a file on the police computer. "Dimanche Diller," he read. "Orphaned daughter of Darcy and Dolores Diller. Brought up by Sisters of Small Mercies until age of three, when claimed by false aunt."

The Chief Inspector blushed. He felt that he was partly to blame for all that had followed. And now it seemed that Dimanche was in danger again. Barry Bullpit rubbed his chin and thought hard. "At least it can't have anything to do with the aunt this time," he remarked to himself. "She's safely behind bars."

He phoned his wife to say he wouldn't be home for tea, and hurried off to the station to buy a ticket to Hilton in the Hollow.

Eight

Tom Shovel stood by his bicycle, saying goodnight to Lucasta Lovelace, his friend and Scrabble partner. The rain fell in cold sheets and the moon turned the road ahead of him to silver whenever it found a gap in the storm clouds. Behind Lucasta's cottage* the floody Fenny foamed and frothed. Tom pulled his hat down over his eyes and buttoned up his mackintosh. "Quartz," he marvelled."You would get quartz, Lucasta." Lucasta smiled.

Tom and Lucasta had been sweethearts years ago, when they were young, but Lucasta had found village life too quiet, and had run away to sea. She had fetched up in Georgetown, Guyana, and headed south and west into the great Amazon Basin. There she had spent many interesting years living among the shy and secret people of that region, absorbing what she could of their vast stores of knowledge.

By the time she returned to her cottage, Tom Shovel was set in his ways. He saw no reason to change them by giving up the freedom of a bachelor life. He and Lucasta met most weeks to share a bottle of cowslip wine and a game or two of scrabble, and parted, happy to see one another but pleased to go their own ways too.

As Tom pedalled slowly away through the rain, thinking about old times, Lucasta Lovelace was making her way down to the little boathouse on the river. She kept a narrowboat there, the *Amazon Queen*. Every summer she would set off down the Fenny, sometimes reaching the great salt estuary before the autumn mists turned her back towards her cottage. The night being so rough, she wanted to make sure the *Amazon Queen* was safe. She was in for a nasty surprise.

Thunder still rumbled, and the odd tongue of lightning licked between the clouds. Tom Shovel, on his bicycle, was thinking of the river too, but he had fishing, not boats, on his mind. He'd have liked to try his luck while the fish were stirred up by the flood water. He sighed happily, remembering the fly-tying kit his grandfather had given him for his tenth birthday.

Just then the moon came out from behind a cloud and something caught Tom's eye. Something shining on the road at the very edge. He got off his bike to have a closer look.

"Well I never!" he exclaimed. "If that ain't Miss Dimanche's penknife!" He tucked it away in his waistcoat pocket, mounted his bike, and pedalled thoughtfully over to Hilton Hall.

When he got home he found a familiar person in an old coat and hat sitting in the moonlight on his back step, smoking a pipe. Close by, an old roan pony cropped and munched on Tom's overgrown lawn.

"Evening, Long Tom," Tom Shovel said as he got off his bike. "I thought that I might find you here. You've heard about young Dimanche then? I found her penknife, on the Rockford Market road, and called in at the Hall to return it. They're in a state up there. They've had a note left on their doorstep, wrapped around Miss Dimanche's pendant. It says she's been captured."

"Is that what it is? I felt in my bones that something was wrong, Tom Shovel. So I rode over, to see if I was wanted."

"Travellers arrived in the valley last night," Tom remarked. "Will you pay 'em a visit, Long Tom?"

"I will, Tom Shovel. You go back the way you came, and wake Lucasta Lovelace. We'll need her help before the night is out."

Tom Shovel climbed rather stiffly onto his bicycle and pedalled back the way he'd come, while Papa Fettler rode away up the valley on his old pony.

Papa Fettler had been friends with the travellers for as long as they'd been coming to the valley. He'd often park his caravan alongside theirs, and spend a week or two with them. Sometimes he took a fancy to go off travelling with them for six months or a year. His closest friend among them was an old, old woman.

More than a hundred years old, her relations said she was. Of course, they may have been boasting, but it's true she looked a hundred, and Papa Fettler had known her a longish while. She had white hair which she kept in two tight plaits that reached below her knees. She wore a heavy overcoat, summer and winter, because old bones feel the cold. She had gold rings in her ears and rubies on her fingers, and a neat little pipe of dark brown wood in which she smoked a selection of herbs. Her name was Thurso.

It's said the travelling people can see the future, cast spells, charm warts, and talk to horses. Whether that is true or not, Thurso often knew things that other people didn't, and Papa Fettler spent an anxious half hour in his old friend's bender. She sat with her back to him, hunched over something precious that she held in her lap. Every now and then she sighed deeply. Evidently she did not like what she saw.

"Flames," she murmured. "Murdering flames. Poor child. Poor, motherless child."

Perhaps it was as well that Papa Fettler could not see into the crystal ball too. If he had, he would have seen, deep in its cold clear heart, red flames licking hungrily around a small and lonely prisoner. And someone with a cruel face striding towards Hilton in the Hollow woods. And a deserted mill beside the flooded Fenny.

When Thurso turned back to Papa Fettler her face was most unhappy. "May you be lucky, old friend," she said. "For the sake of that poor child. Lucky and quick, Papa Fettler."

nine

Deep in the woods, the charcoal-burner's shack trembled under the onslaught of the storm. Thunder ripped across the sky. Lightning alternately revealed and hid the ragged tree tops, making them jump and flicker. Inside the cottage Dimanche sat, pale and still, on the chair to which Wolfie had tied her.

Polly Cockle had taught Dimanche, when she was just a little girl, that poetry can be a comfort in time of trouble, and she decided to keep up her spirits by reciting one of her favourites.

"Then out spake brave Horatius,"

she began in a small but steady voice,

"The Captain of the Gate:
'To every man upon this earth
Death cometh soon or late;
And how can man die better
Than facing fearful odds
For the ashes of his fathers
And the temples of his Gods',"

Dimanche felt courage flowing back into her veins. She sat up straight, and had just begun on the next verse, when her words were drowned by a peal of thunder which seemed to bounce down the dark sky and land on the very roof of the house. Ceiling, walls, and floor rocked. A sound like stiff paper crumpling, but a million times louder, split the air. Dimanche crouched as low as she could in her chair, eyes shut, trying not to hear, see, smell, or understand. In vain. A second later bright flickering light and the smell of burning told her the worst had happened. Lightning had struck the cottage, shattering the slates and setting light to the rafters beneath. Over her head, the lath and plaster ceiling began to pop and crackle. Dimanche understood all too well the deadly peril of her situation. She was alone, a prisoner with no hope of escape, trapped in a burning house.

It is the smoke that is the deadliest danger in a burning house, and already dark swirls of smoke were billowing down from the rafters, coiling themselves round Dimanche's head. Even as she began to choke, she realized that the air might be breathable down by the floor. With one tremendous effort she rocked her chair right over, skinning her knees and banging her elbows, but bringing her face down to the bare boards.

Oily black fumes quickly filled the upper half of the little room. The tar paper that had been laid under the roof slates rained down in burning rags and tatters all round where she lay, giving off noxious fumes and starting new, small fires in the floorboards close by. Dimanche shut her eyes and began to rock her chair again, sliding it inch by inch under the table. The table top was white enamel. It might protect her from the fiery debris for a while, if she could only get under it.

Just as she got her head and shoulders in under the table, a cascade of burning rafters fell into the room. Thick smoke swirled close to Dimanche's face, stinging her nose, her eyes, her throat. She tried to hold her breath, but nobody can do that for long. Out it came in a great heaving gasp and the very next instant she would have had to fill her lungs with suffocating smoke. In the tiny space of time between Dimanche breathing out and breathing in, the cottage door burst open and a glistening creature, coated in a thick dark substance, hurled itself across the room.

It was Wolfie T. Volfango. He had fallen into the river on his way back from delivering Dimanche's note to Hilton Hall and in climbing out had covered himself all over in glutinous black mud. And it was this that enabled him to rescue Dimanche. Fiery debris rained down on him as he stood, dumbstruck, staring into the flame-filled room.

Burning bits fell on him, hissed on contact with the slimy mud, and went out. He could not see Dimanche, whose feet were the only part of her still sticking out from under the enamel-topped table, but he could hear her all right.

Bending down to peer under the table, Wolfie came nose to nose with her. With one hand he cast aside the kitchen table and with the other swept up Dimanche, along with the chair to which she was still tied. Clasping her to his muddy chest, he raced from the burning cottage. No sooner had Wolfie and Dimanche cleared the door frame than the roof collapsed. Sparks and flames shot upwards, hissing in the rain. Within minutes the cottage was a fiercely burning shell.

"Thank you, Wolfie," said Dimanche sarcastically. "Now perhaps you would untie me?"

Wolfie nodded miserably. He had never meant to hurt Dimanche. He looked across at the fiery remains of the charcoal-burner's shack and his hands shook so much that he could not get his own knots undone. He had just cut the first of the knots in half, using his mighty

hunter sheath knife, when out of the thick belt
of holly trees jumped a tall figure dressed in
prison dungarees.

Ten

"So. Untying the prisoner, are you, Wolfie? Now why would you do a stupid thing like that? Don't you know she's as slippery as a serpent?"

Wolfie's eyes widened in horrified surprise. "Auntie!" he gasped. "What are you doing here? Why aren't you still in prison?"

Dimanche said nothing. She had fainted, as people do sometimes immediately after they have been in great danger. She lay still on the wet grass, trailing rope and knots. As Wolfie looked at her, he felt a change happening inside himself. It was something to do with the way he felt about Dimanche. What happened to her suddenly seemed to matter more than what his aunt might do to him.

"You didn't imagine that I'd trust you to do the business on your own, did you, Wolfie?" his aunt continued.

"I was doin' all right, Auntie."

"All right? *All right*? What would you call doing badly? You have set fire to the house in which you were supposed to keep your hostage hidden. The flames are rising twenty feet high into the sky. You might as well have written a message in fireworks saying *Here we are*! And I don't suppose you've even delivered the ransom demand yet. You are an idiot, Wolfie! What are you?"

Wolfie shuffled his feet uncomfortably and looked at Dimanche. She was just coming round and beginning to sit up and rub where the ropes had made her arms sore. She took one look at Wolfie's aunt and fainted dead away again. Wolfie shook his head.

"I've took a note, Auntie. I've took a note to

the big house sayin' Dimanche is all right. So her auntie an' all won't be worried."

"You've done *what*, you *nincompoop*??? We want her auntie to be worried! We want all of them to be worried sick! That's why we kidnapped the brat. To scare them into paying us a fortune. If they're not worried, why would they pay up? You're even stupider than Gussie said you were! You're a complete and utter fool! I don't see how even my dumb sister could have had a son like you!"

Poor Wolfie hung his head. Dimanche had come round again and was staring open-mouthed at Wolfie's aunt. For a moment she was absolutely speechless with surprise. Because Wolfie's aunt was no stranger to her. No stranger at all.

"Valburga Vilemile!" she gasped. "You're supposed to be in prison! You're Wolfie's beastly aunt! You told him to kidnap me! Well, now you can just shut up! Wolfie's not stupid and brainless, he's just nicer than you are, so jolly well leave him alone, you rotten bully!"

"Don't take that tone with me, you little guttersnipe!" Valburga hissed. "It's time you learned to treat your elders and betters with respect. And I'm the one to teach you how!"

"Elder yes, better no!" shouted Dimanche. "You can't teach me anything I want to know! Untie me, Wolfie."

Nobody had ever told Wolfie that he was nice. Nobody had ever called him anything but stupid. His mother was horrible, just like his aunt, and he had never known his father. He had no brothers or sisters or even cousins to stand up for him. On top of that, when Wolfie was at school his teachers used to say things like: "Wolfie simply doesn't try," or else, "That Wolfie is bone idle."

Wolfie's childhood had not been a happy one, and what he felt about himself was not the pleasant, proud sort of feeling a person should feel. Mostly he felt a sad and gloomy I'm-no-good-at-anything feeling. And now Dimanche was telling his mean old auntie that he wasn't stupid! Telling her he was NICE! Ignoring his venomous aunt, Wolfie bent over Dimanche, and shook her politely by the hand.

"I'm sorry I kidnapped you, Dimanche," he said.

"Well, you didn't, exactly. I tripped over you, if you remember. I suppose you kidnapped me after that, but you'd never have caught me if I hadn't got tangled up in your sleeping bag. And you did take the message to Hilton Hall. And after that you saved my life. You're OK, Wolfie. Now get on and untie me."

Wolfie blushed. "Sure thing, Dimanche," he murmured. "Right away."

"Oh no you don't, Wolfie T. Volfango!" snarled Valburga. "You seem to be forgetting I'm in charge here! And I didn't waste my time in prison. No. I learnt many interesting and useful skills there. Skills I knew would come in useful on the outside. Take hypnosis."

"I'd rather not, Auntie," said Wolfie nervously.

"I couldn't care less what you'd rather!" snapped his aunt. "Look into my eyes!"

Wolfie did. He couldn't help himself. Valburga's eyes were cold and still, with no real expression in them, just a shifting pulse of horrid cruelty at the back of them. Her pupils were dull and black, rather like tadpoles. Wolfie could hear her voice saying something, but it seemed to be coming from a long way off. He remembered that he'd felt like this before, when the dentist had given him an injection. This time, it was his Aunt Valburga who was somehow sending him to sleep. He shook his head slowly but it didn't help. He felt completely muddled up.

"Wolfie T. Volfango," said Valburga. "You will do exactly as I tell you. You will obey my every command. Do you understand me, Wolfie?"

Wolfie nodded.

"What are you going to do, Wolfie?"

"I'm gonna obey your every command," droned Wolfie.

Valburga Vilemile smiled a happy smile and turned towards Dimanche. "Now for you, Miss Troublemaker!" she said.

Dimanche shut her eyes tightly. "I'm not listening to you," she said, "and I'm not looking into your eyes."

"Suit yourself," Valburga replied. "I just thought you might like to hear what I'm going to do with your stupid friend."

"I'm still not listening," Dimanche said. But she was.

"Fine," smiled Valburga. "I don't need him, you see, because I've got you now. And I think he could be quite a nuisance. He never was quick on the uptake, and I've got better things to do than trail him through the woods all night. So I'm going to tell him to walk right into the middle of the River Fenny. And sit down. That should be interesting, don't you think?"

"No!" shouted Dimanche. "You can't! You mustn't!" She scrambled to her feet, and stared in horror at Valburga Vilemile. Which was exactly what Valburga had intended.

Valburga's cold eyes bored into her victim's brain. Dimanche felt Valburga's loveless world trickling out of those dull black pupils, deadening her own lively brain. Far down inside her, her own true self remained, steadfast and strong. But round and over it crept the frozen slush of Valburga's hypnotic power. It spread, and settled like lava. Within seconds, Dimanche was Valburga's slave.

Valburga smiled. She took Wolfie's prized sheath knife and sliced through Dimanche's remaining knots. "Right," she said. "That's that. Now link arms, and do exactly as I say. Walk!"

Dimanche and Wolfie shuffled off. It was a strange, unpleasant feeling. The prisoners could see, and feel, and hear, and speak, but an invisible force-field of icy power kept them subdued to their captor's wishes. It soon became obvious to them that they were being led straight to the flooded Fenny Water, out of which poor Wolfie had only just climbed. It crossed Dimanche's mind that Valburga might be planning to give up on the ransom and drown the evidence. Their bodies would never be found. The swirling currents would wash them down to the great salt sea, where the fishes would dispose of them. If only somebody knew where we are, Dimanche thought wretchedly. If only somebody could see us.

Nobody did. Nobody could. Except for one old woman, staring anxiously into a crystal ball.

Eleven

The rush and tumble of the Fenny Water soon filled the prisoners' ears. Normally a quiet, peat-brown stream sliding secretly through woods and fields, it had been changed entirely by the storm water that overflowed its banks. It bubbled and boiled like water in a kettle. Tiny salmon fry, new hatched, were tossed about like silver pins. Little brown elvers coiled and moiled joyfully in the swirls and eddies, and a fleet of Aylesbury ducks dived and swam in the foam. The scene would usually have pleased Dimanche, but being a prisoner, and hypnotized, took all the fun away.

"Follow the bank upstream!" Valburga snapped. "And get a move on! We haven't got all night."

Dimanche and Wolfie stumbled forward, water swishing round their ankles, rain wetting their necks and blowing up their sleeves. Presently the woods gave way to open fields. All the low-lying ground was flooded, trees grew straight up out of the water, and silver bubbles of air beaded the grass. A little further up, the Fenny opened out into a pool. Beside it were some tumbledown warehouses and half an old boathouse, left over from the days when barges used to come up-river.

Dimanche wondered if Valburga was going to let them stop, to rest and shelter from the storm. She hoped so. She had been chased, caught, tied up, trapped in a burning building, rescued, hypnotised, and marched through a flood all in one night, and she was almost exhausted.

They passed the tumbledown sheds and turned off at the boathouse.

"Get inside!" Valburga ordered. Dimanche stumbled forward. Wolfie did his best to give her an encouraging smile, but it came out all crumpled. Together they half-walked, half-fell into the boathouse and sank down on a pile of old tarpaulins to rest. "Get up!" Valburga barked. "I didn't say you could sit down! Get up and get on board!"

Dimanche stared round her in the darkness. There had never been a boat in here. Not a proper one, that you could get on board. There had been a completely rotten rowing boat one summer, when she was little. She had played pirates in it, and eaten picnics beside it, but it had disappeared ages ago, taken for firewood by a passing tramp.

Valburga lit a lamp and in the beam of its light Dimanche could see, rocking on the black water, a neat little boat that she knew well. The *Amazon Queen*, Lucasta Lovelace's pride and joy. Dimanche and Wolfie scrambled aboard the narrow boat with Valburga right behind them.

"Untie that painter and cast off!" she ordered. Wolfie obeyed. The little boat's engine responded instantly to Valburga's finger on the button and she swung out into the current and set off bobbing and bouncing upstream.

The *Amazon Queen* was a beauty. There were two little bench seats of polished wood, with velvet cushions, which turned into bunk beds. There were cupboards full of interesting bottles and canisters. There was a tiny stove with pots and pans and a chimney pipe that went up through the deck. There were proper little windows with curtains, and some rather good etchings of the Fenny Water through the seasons, made by Lucasta's father.

Valburga Vilemile noticed none of this. She had no eye for beauty. She pushed her prisoners down on one of the bench seats, keeping them covered with a wicked stare. She ordered Dimanche to draw the curtains and light a candle. Then she took out a map and studied it briefly.

"Right," she said. "You two go for'ard and make sure we don't run foul of floating debris or low bridges. If the boat sinks, you sink with it, so keep it floating. I'm going to sit here, cosy and dry, with my feet up. But I'll be watching you."

So it was that under cover of darkness the *Amazon Queen* bobbed up the flooded Fenny, while Dimanche and Wolfie kept her as close to mid-stream as they could. Now and then they fended off a floating log or pushed off from the bank. Each time they glanced back at Valburga, she was sitting with her muddy feet up on Lucasta's velvet cushions, and her elbows on the table. Her cold eyes stared at them in a way that made them forget all their thoughts, feelings, hopes and fears, and concentrate only on her selfish wishes.

Twelve

Morning found Dimanche, Wolfie and Valburga tying up at Miller's Reach. Valburga made her prisoners hide the *Amazon Queen* as best they could behind the ruined mill.

While Dimanche was sitting in the ruined mill, thinking sad and muddled thoughts, the world outside was waking up, and feeling itself to see if it was still in one piece after the storm. The sun rose into a sky of storm-washed green, polishing the Fenny valley with a wintry sheen. It shone in at one broken doorway of the ruined mill and out at the other. Each door had the remains of a little fanlight over its lintel. In olden days the miller would have watched the sun rise in one, and seen it set in the other.

Further up the Fenny the Aylesbury ducks flapped their wings and enjoyed their seasonal feast of elvers. Presently something on the river bank disturbed them. Three figures were creeping silently towards the ruined mill. The ducks stopped scoffing and took to their wings, flying low because of being full of baby eels.

Valburga meanwhile was clinking something in the pockets of her dungarees. She fished out two sets of shiny new handcuffs, two lengths of chain, and two heavy padlocks. She set one of each down on the ground beside her prisoners. Then, with an extra powerful stare, she ordered Wolfie to handcuff Dimanche, and chain her to the bars of an old manger. Next, Wolfie was told to sit with his back to the great millstone which lay half hidden in the earth. Sunk deep into the stone was a big iron ring. Dimanche had noticed it the last time she was here. Papa Fettler had told her what it was.

"Been there a good few years, that ring has,"

he had said. "After this place stopped being a working mill, a farmer had that ring set in that stone. He owned the biggest, heaviest bull in the country, a champion creature, gentle unless roused. If anything upset him, there was hell to pay. Nothing and nobody could hold that bull. In the end the farmer had the ring set in the millstone and chained the creature to it. It wasn't such a bad life for a bull. He had the shelter of the barn, and the farmer made sure his chain was good and long so he could go outside and eat grass when he wanted to. Folks felt safer once that bull was chained."

To this very ring now Valburga Vilemile chained her nephew, Wolfie. She didn't have a scrap of family feeling. She simply locked his padlock and tossed his key and Dimanche's into the river. Then she took a sheet of paper and a biro from her pocket. This is what she wrote:

Dear Sister Victorine,

I have your nasty little niece, Dimanche. She is my prisoner, and I have chained her up somewhere you'll never find her. If you want her back, put £20,000 into a sack, and leave it in the ruins of the charcoal-burner's shack.

I shall be leaving the country shortly.
When I have done so, with the money, I will let
you know where you can find your niece. If the
money is not in the sack, or if anyone tries to
watch or follow me, or if I fail to arrive at my
chosen destination with the money, you will
receive no further instructions.

I should warn you that if she is not found
within three days or so, your niece is unlikely
to be found alive. There will be a young man
with her. He is a criminal and ought to be
locked up. If he says he's a relation of mine,
he's lying.

Yours faithfully,
VALBURGA VILEMILE.

When Valburga had finished her letter, she
stood up and looked around the ruined mill.
Satisfied that there was absolutely no escape for
either of her prisoners, she went on board the
Amazon Queen and cooked herself a large
breakfast. Then she made herself a pot of
coffee, drank it, threw her dirty plate and cup
into the river so as not to have the bother of

washing them up, and strolled back into the mill. Bending down in front of first Wolfie, then Dimanche, she snapped her fingers in their faces.

At once the frozen lava melted and flowed away, and Dimanche was her own self once more, with only a dim and muddled memory of how she came to be in the ruined mill, chained to the bars of a manger. Wolfie could remember nothing after seeing his aunt loom up out of the darkness beside the charcoal-burner's shack.

Valburga smiled at her prisoners. "I'm off now," she said. "If your precious Sister Verity does as she's told, Dimanche, someone may come and get you. In a week or so. If not, they won't. Don't bother shouting. Nobody will hear you. And don't think old Papa Fettler will come by with his stupid horse and cart, because the roads are three foot under water. It'll be prison for you, Wolfie, when they find you. If they find you. By the time you get out, I shall be far away. You won't find me, so don't bother looking. We could have had a partnership, if you'd played your cards right. Too bad you didn't."

"You wouldn't have shared the money with

me anyway, Auntie," Wolfie said. "I wouldn't have shared it with you, either. I used to be just like you, so I know. But I'm not any more."

"You can say that again," Valburga chuckled. "I'm free and rich. You're flat broke and handcuffed to a millwheel."

Thirteen

When Valburga stopped speaking, silence fell over the ruined mill. Silence, apart from the gentle lap of the Fenny and the quiet creak of the *Amazon Queen* rocking on her moorings.

A tremor of anxiety brushed across Valburga's mind. She turned slowly to cross the space that lay between herself and the east door. As she did so, a tall, bent figure, black against the rosy morning sky, stepped into view, and Valburga found herself staring into old Tom Shovel's angry face.

"If you've harmed Miss Dimanche," he growled, "you're going to wish you hadn't."

"Who's going to make me wish that, old man?" Valburga mocked.

"I am," came a quiet voice from the west door.

There in the doorway stood Lucasta Lovelace, a deadly blowpipe to her lips. She made a quiet sound, like a jaguar coughing in a rain forest. A tiny dart flew from the hollow pipe and lodged itself in the back of Valburga's neck.

During her time with the Indians of the Amazon Basin, Lucasta had spent long hours studying the rare and deadly poisons used by those resourceful people. She had brought back with her a precious store of ingredients, animal, vegetable and mineral, out of which she could concoct poisons for all occasions. For years she had longed to put her skills to the test, but there is very little opportunity, in a quiet English village, for testing poisoned darts. She couldn't help feeling delighted to find Valburga Vilemile in her sights.

The poison started to work as soon as the dart had pierced Valburga's skin. A look of surprise crossed her face. That is, it began to cross it, but then it froze. One half of Valburga's face wore an angry, telling-off expression, while the other half looked amazed. Then her whole body seemed to solidify, as if cement had filled her veins. She stood, furious and astonished, her arms outstretched, rather like a signpost. The poison was already working on her knees, neither of which could now be moved. Her feet shuffled uncertainly as the poison coursed round her ankles, then they too succumbed. She stood stock-still, shades of red and green washing alternately across her face. Outwardly, she didn't move a muscle, but the sheer force of her emotion toppled her gently sideways and she fell with a gentle thump onto the damp earth floor.

"How are the mighty fallen," Lucasta breathed happily. "Will you look at that, Tom? Perfect, eh?"

Tom nodded admiringly. "Ten out of ten, Lucasta," he beamed.

"Is she dead?" Dimanche asked hopefully.

"Just paralysed," Lucasta told her. "And it's

only temporary. We must keep an eye on her to see that she doesn't choke. The poison should wear off in exactly seven minutes, if I judged the dose correctly."

"Lucasta, you're a marvel," Tom said, kissing her hand.

"Very nicely done, Lucasta," Papa Fettler agreed, leading old Rosie in through the broken doorway.

"Oh, it was nothing really. Let's get the young ones loose, and tie the old bat up."

"How did you know we were here, Lucasta?" Dimanche asked. "And how are you going to set us free, now that you've found us? We're handcuffed, chained and padlocked. Valburga threw the keys into the river."

"Papa Fettler will explain how we found you. And young Wolfie will set you free."

"Me?" asked Wolfie. "How?"

"Easy. That ring was only made to hold a raging bull. A lad like you will have no trouble with it."

Wolfie nodded. He flexed his muscles, and did some deep breathing. He began to strain with all the strength of his mighty biceps. Leaning in towards the millstone to exert maximum leverage, he grasped the chain in both hands – not easy when you're handcuffed – and began to heave. Sweat formed on his forehead and dripped down into his eyes. He grunted fiercely. The veins on his temples bulged and throbbed. The muscles of his arms and back swelled to the size of pumpkins. Dimanche, Lucasta and Tom watched intently as slowly, and with a noise like grinding teeth, the iron ring tore from the millstone.

All in one moment, the ring flew out, the handcuffs flew into a dozen pieces, and Wolfie flew backwards across the room and landed triumphantly on top of his Aunt Valburga. Tom and Lucasta gave him a round of applause. Dimanche would have liked to join in, but you can't clap when you're handcuffed to a manger. Wolfie picked himself up, said sorry to his aunt, and bowed to his audience.

"Your turn now, Dimanche," he grunted. Carefully, so as not to do any more damage than was strictly necessary, he pulled the manger out of the wall and slid Dimanche's chain free. Delicately, but with immense strength, he prised her handcuffs open.

"Thank you, Wolfie, you're a real hero,"

Dimanche said. She kissed him on both cheeks, French-style.

"Aw shucks," said Wolfie happily.

There was no time for further pleasantries. Valburga Vilemile was beginning to twitch like a sack of eels on the floor of the old mill.

"Quick," Lucasta shouted. "Fetch rope from the boat and tie her up!"

Fourteen

What joy there was at Hilton Hall when Papa Fettler, Tom Shovel, Lucasta Lovelace and Dimanche, accompanied unwillingly by Valburga Vilemile, now secured by a length of her own chain, staggered up the steps and in through the front door. Only Barry Bullpit, bustling around his prisoner, was not entirely happy. He was disappointed for two reasons. One – he hadn't had time to mount a proper search party before the missing person returned. And two –

although he now had the pleasure of arresting Valburga Vilemile, her nephew Wolfie seemed to have got clean away.

"I don't know how he got away from us," Tom Shovel said. "Well, I do. He ran. But we weren't expecting him to, you see. So we didn't try to stop him. If you catch my meaning, Chief Inspector."

"We thought he was going to come back with us and hand himself over," Papa Fettler agreed, "him being such a nice young lad."

Dimanche said nothing. There was nothing she could say. Aiding and abetting a criminal to escape is an offence, and Dimanche knew it. Since she had no intention of incriminating herself, she had to keep quiet, because she simply could not bring herself to say anything that would get Wolfie into trouble.

"What are you going to do, Wolfie?" she had asked as they trudged along behind old Rose. "Will you give yourself up?"

"Nope."

"But Wolfie, shouldn't you?"

"You know my auntie, Dimanche. She'll put all the blame on me. I'll be sent down for a hundred years. Well, I'm not going! I want my freedom! I got to find out who I am, an' what it all means, an' such like. An' no aunt is going to stop me."

"But where will you go, Wolfie? What will you do?"

"I'll live in your woods, if you don't mind, Dimanche. Sleep out under the stars. Forage for my food. Build things."

"Build things, Wolfie? What things? Dens?"

Wolfie shook his head. His small eyes shone with happiness. "Not dens, Dimanche," he said. "Airplanes!"

"But Wolfie! How?"

"You seen what I can do with a piece of rope. I'm sorry I did that, now, 'course I am, but tell me honestly, what am I like at knots?"

"You're brilliant, Wolfie."

Wolfie nodded modestly. "I'm good at 'em because I like 'em. I like rope and string and such. Always have done. And elastic bands. And I like flying. Well. That's not how it is, Dimanche. I don't just *like* flying. I want to fly so bad I could just about grow wings."

"Are you going to build a sort of flying machine? Out in the woods?"

"That's about it, Dimanche!"

"Oh, Wolfie! I'll help you all I can. I'll bring you stuff you need, and food, and treats when I can save enough pocket money. What sort of sweets do you like best?"

"Gum."

"Right."

Wolfie and Dimanche looked at one another. Both of them knew that there, on the muddy path across the fields, a life-long friendship had begun.

"Make a run for it, Wolfie," Dimanche advised. And Wolfie did.

Inspector Bullpit never found him. Once or twice he stumbled on a hide-out or a den. Once, and this he found unbearably exciting, he found a fire still smouldering, where Wolfie had been toasting marshmallows. But Wolfie was too quick for Barry Bullpit. He'd hear him coming, and he'd run for cover. Eventually the inspector had to admit defeat, and go back to London. But the case has never been closed.

Even Verity Victorine and Polly Cockle don't know exactly where Dimanche goes on her long, solitary walks. They know she takes supplies with her, some most peculiar ones. Quantities of string, sometimes, and a great deal of chewing gum, which she herself has never liked. Each of them has her suspicions. But they do not speak of them to one another.

Sometimes Dimanche takes her one-man tent, and walks deep into the woods. She stops, and makes a secret signal. Presently she hears Wolfie crashing through the undergrowth. She and Wolfie light a campfire, and cook things, and talk late into the night. Wolfie rolls into his all-weather duckdown sleeping bag, and Dimanche crawls into her one-man tent. They listen to the night noises that no longer frighten Wolfie, and dream their separate dreams.

Sometimes, out in the woods, Dimanche finds a complicated contraption made of wood and string and feathers, bits of old tarpaulin, wire, large leaves, elastic bands. It makes her happy when she does, because she knows that Wolfie is still trying to fly.

Perhaps, one day, he will.

Henrietta Branford

Dimanche Diller

Smarties Book Prize Winner
Shortlisted for the Guardian Award

"What children want is squashing down! What children want is flattening out!"

Would you want a guardian who said that? Dimanche Diller certainly didn't, but she had one anyway – called Valburga Vilemile! And Valburga has more than a squashing planned for Dimanche. After all, it's only Dimanche who stands in the way of what Valburga wants above everything else – Hilton Hall and the Diller family fortune. But Dimanche isn't easy to defeat – so who will flatten who?

" A galloping story of escape and adventure." *Guardian*